Licensed exclusively to Top That Publishing Ltd
Tide Mill Way, Woodbridge, Suffolk, IP12 1AP, UK
www.topthatpublishing.com
Copyright © 2016 Tide Mill Media
All rights reserved
2 4 6 8 9 7 5 3 1
Manufactured in China

Retold by Oakley Graham
Illustrated by Rosie Butcher

ISBN 978-1-78700-008-7

A catalogue record for this book is available from the British Library

Hans Christian Andersen's

The Snow Queen

Retold by Oakley Graham

Illustrated by Rosie Butcher

Once upon a time there lived a wicked troll king who built a magic mirror. The mirror made anything that was beautiful or good look ugly and bad in its reflection.

The troll king was very mean indeed! He travelled around the world and used the mirror to make people see the worst in everything and everyone.

One day, the troll king decided to make fun of the angels by showing them their reflection in his mirror. But, as he tried to carry the mirror towards the heavens, he dropped it and the mirror shattered into a million tiny pieces!

A strong wind picked up the magic mirror
pieces and blew them all over the Earth ...

Tiny fragments of mirror
were blown into people's eyes,
making them see the world
as a foul and rotten place,
and when a mirror fragment
touched someone's heart
it froze them hard
like ice, so they
no longer felt joy.

Years later, pieces of the mirror fell in a small town where two best friends, Kai and Gerda, lived happily. As the friends read a book together, a splinter of broken mirror flew into Kai's eye and another pierced his heart!

In an instant, everything changed …

Kai destroyed the roses he and Gerda had planted together, and he argued and taunted her over the smallest of things. Soon, the friends rarely played together any more.

The next winter, Kai was playing alone in the snow when a giant carriage drew up beside him. The mysterious driver called Kai over, and he found himself staring into the piercing blue eyes of the Snow Queen!

Kai was spellbound, and when the Snow Queen invited
him to ride with her he was powerless to resist.

Kai was fearful and numb with the cold.
Seeing that he was afraid, the Snow Queen
kissed him on the forehead.

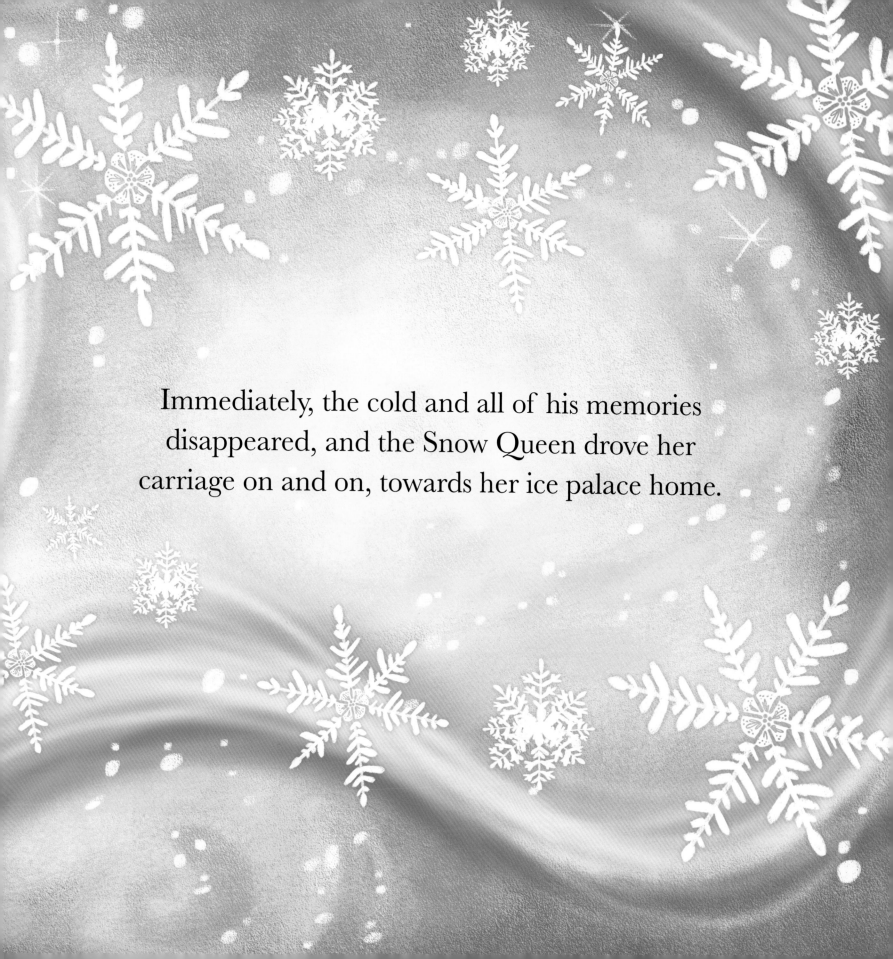

Immediately, the cold and all of his memories disappeared, and the Snow Queen drove her carriage on and on, towards her ice palace home.

When Kai did not return home, the people of the town thought that he must have drowned in the river, but his loyal friend, Gerda, felt sure that he was still alive.

First, Gerda took her boat to the river and offered her new shoes as a gift if the river returned her friend. But the river did not have Kai, so Gerda continued with her search.

Next, Gerda's search took her to an enchanted garden of eternal summer. The fairy who owned the garden was very lonely, so she cast a magic spell to make Gerda forget everything and stay! As the spell took hold, all of the roses in the garden sank below the ground, so that Gerda would not be reminded of home and Kai.

As time passed, Gerda could not understand why she felt so sad in such a beautiful place. Then one day, as she wept, one of her tears touched the ground and a rose bush sprang up. The flowers whispered to Gerda that Kai was not dead, and with that the fairy's spell was broken!

Gerda escaped from the enchanted garden, and after walking for many miles she met a raven. By now, Gerda was very hungry, so she was grateful when the kind raven gave her some bread. As Gerda ate, she told the raven all about the search for her friend.

The raven listened carefully. Then he told Gerda about a princess and her quest to find a husband who was both clever and funny. The princess had found her perfect prince, and the raven believed that the prince might be Kai!

Gerda was excited by the raven's news, and went in search of the princess's palace. But when she arrived, she discovered that the prince the raven spoke about was not her dear friend after all.

The prince and princess felt very sorry for Gerda, so they gave her some warm clothes and a fine carriage, so that she could continue her search.

Not long after Gerda left the palace, robbers spied her fancy carriage and attacked it! Luckily, a little robber girl took pity on Gerda, so the other robbers did not harm her and took her back to their hideout.

There, the little robber girl kept wood pigeons and a reindeer tied up as pets. One night, while the little robber girl slept, the raven came to visit Gerda and spoke to the wood pigeons. Cooing quietly, they told the raven that the Snow Queen had taken Kai to Lapland!

In the morning, Gerda told the little
robber girl what the wood pigeons had said.
The little robber girl could see that Gerda
was upset, so she agreed to free her and let
her take the reindeer to ride on.

It was a long journey to the Snow Queen's palace and Gerda made two stops.

The first was at a Lapp woman's home. The Lapp woman told Gerda that the Snow Queen had moved from her summer palace in Lapland, to her winter palace in Finmark.

The second stop was at a Finn woman's home. The Finn woman told the reindeer that the secret of Gerda's special power to save Kai from the Snow Queen was in her innocent child's heart.

When Gerda reached the Snow Queen's palace,
she was stopped by icy snowflakes that were
guarding it. But when she said a prayer,
her breath took the shape of angels,
who battled with the snowflakes so that
she could enter the palace safely.

Once inside, Gerda found Kai all alone on a frozen lake.

Kai was completely still as he sat trying to solve a puzzle that
the Snow Queen had set him. If Kai was able to form the word
'eternity' from splintered pieces of ice, the Snow Queen had
promised to release him from her power.

Gerda was thrilled to see that her friend was alive!
She ran up to Kai and kissed him, crying tears of
happiness. As Gerda's warm tears fell on Kai,
they melted his heart and burnt away the
magic mirror splinter inside.

In an instant, everything changed …

Able to feel once more, Kai began crying too,
and his tears dislodged the splinter from his eye.
Kai was a healthy and happy boy again!

Kai and Gerda danced joyfully on the frozen lake and splinters of ice joined them, spinning, swirling and twirling. When the reunited friends tired of dancing, the ice splinters fell down to spell 'eternity'.

The Snow Queen's spell was broken and Kai was free to return home with his very best friend, Gerda.